NIGHT SWIFTLY FALLING

TRICIA D. WAGNER

LYRIDAE BOOKS

PRAISE FOR TRICIA D. WAGNER

"*NIGHT SWIFTLY FALLING* IS ONE OF THE MOST CLEVER, CONTEMPLATIVE BOOKS I'VE READ ALL SUMMER. IN ADDITION TO A TIGHTLY WOVEN PLOT, THE AUTHOR DEMONSTRATES A MASTERFUL COMMAND OF THE LANGUAGE IN EVERY PARAGRAPH THAT'LL KEEP YOU TURNING PAGES UNTIL THE END.

PROPELLED BY DELICIOUS PROSE, *NIGHT SWIFTLY FALLING* IS POIGNANT AND HEARTFELT. THIS BEAUTIFULLY WRITTEN NOVELETTE, HONEST AND HOPEFUL ALL AT THE SAME TIME, PACKS A PUNCH. AN EXCEPTIONAL ACHIEVEMENT."

-KRISTINE L., REVIEWER, REEDSY DISCOVERY

Go you must.
No guest will stay in one place forever.
Love will be lost if you sit too long at a friend's fire.

The Havamal
Old Norse Song of the High One

I

I come out of hiding, from among the jumble of foremast ropes on my father's ship.

Crossing the deck of his brigantine—the *Regulus*, is a risk. That scallywag promenading as the good and upright fishing lad— Johnny Minnow—could be bunkering anyplace. And he knows I'm onto him.

But the deck remains empty and quiet, except for the whistling of Captain Justus (my father, good natured enough to don a feathered pirate cap for the ride home, to make things feel more epic).

The sun beats on my bare shoulders, and the rock of the boat on this blue Celtic water feels like the dancing of the Earth. Its rhythm is even and cool. No drumbeat of scampering footsteps troubles the deck.

Empress Adara and Caius the Magistrate, along for the sailing trip, are resting at the stern of the ship, watching the shore come. They seem oblivious that dark deeds are astir.

"Steady as she goes, Swift," my father, Justus, calls to me, playing his role well enough. Though, he's forgotten that I'm not plain "Swift" at the moment, but the dauntless ocean adventurer—Captain Swift Corkscrew—a privateer, fearless in the face of all wrongdoing; a buccaneer resolute to make good on my oath to Empress Adara and set this sea safe from all piracy.

"Keep a weather eye on the horizon," says Captain Justus.

But I can't mind my post of lookout right now. Not when foul acts of treason and pillaging have been committed by that picaroon, "Johnny Minnow," whom I suspect is the dread Captain Ash Coxswain, Pirate Tormenter of the Cold Celtic Sea. I need only find the proof of his deceit.

Captain Justus, wise as he is, doesn't interfere nor does he question my business as I cross the deck and slip furtively into the trap door leading to the galley.

Captain Justus gives me a supportive nod and trains his own gaze on the horizon, where a storm indeed brews.

I close the trap door and slink down the dark ladder.

"I know you're in here, you trickster," I speak to the darkness.

There isn't a sound in reply. Not a breath. Not a stifled laugh. Nothing.

I flick on my flashlight and turn a fast circle, training its beam all around and expecting that artist of duplicity, Johnny Minnow / Ash Coxswain, to leap out with his rapier and slay me.

Ash doesn't leap out, though. He doesn't seem to be anyplace down here.

But. My light brushes something that sparkles.

I kneel before the galley sink and throw back the dishtowel concealing its pipes.

"I knew it," I whisper.

I clench a fistful of wealth from the trove—Monopoly money and glittering coins and real chocolate galleons and jewels so shining they seem made of sugar, and pearls so swollen and glossed they look fake.

"Johnny Minnow claims he's an honest fishing lad," I say. "But here, I find evidence he's telling lies."

I stand, cramming as much of the wealth as possible into my trouser pockets.

A voice hisses from the darkness—"So what if I lied?"

I spin and catch the swipe of a rapier blade on my own.

"I suspected you kept a dark secret." I bear down on the marauder, the swindler. "You're not Johnny Minnow, the jolly fishing lad from bonny Bristol. You're the notorious pirate, Ash Coxswain! Admit it."

With a mighty burst, the false Johnny Minnow throws me back against the sink. "That's Captain Ash Coxswain, Pirate Tormenter of the Cold Celtic Sea."

He's wrapping both his hands around the hilt of his rapier, as though readying to plunge it straight through my body, to fasten my bones to his trove as a trophy—one more of a long line of souls that he's claimed.

Ash lunges—I feign, and I spin—I'm behind him now, clenching him into a headlock and swiping his blade from his hand.

"You think you can get away with murder, don't you?" I ask.

Ash shouts, "I have gotten away with murder."

He struggles to get free, but can't. Ash is shirtless, as I am, and we stick to each other. My arm crossing his chest is as strong as a hawser rope.

"And I'll get away with much worse," says the villain.

Indeed, Ash's elusiveness is his genius. He's clever enough at school to never get caught breaking rules. He even regularly springs me—his best friend—from tight places.

But now it's me, Captain Corkscrew, who's onto him.

"Not this time." I cut free the dishcloth hanging over the sink pipes and, with it, bind his wrists. "Caius the Magistrate is on board," I tell him.

"Cockle shards—not Caius the Magistrate!" Ash squirms. "Please, I'll do anything. I'll give you half of what I've plundered. Just don't deliver me to Caius the Magistrate."

But the famed luck of the notorious Captain Ash Coxswain has run out, because the galley trap door is opening.

And at its brink stands the right noble Caius the Magistrate.

"We'll be docking in a few minutes," says Caius. "You lads want to watch me lower the sails?"

Ordinarily, we would. But now that I've proven who our dear and doe-eyed Johnny Minnow really is, there are more important matters at hand.

"Let me watch him work the sails one last time," says Ash. "Before I'm condemned."

"Quiet, you!" I haul him to the ladder and force him to its top under the threat of a blade to his bottom.

"You'll never believe it," I tell Caius the Magistrate, once Ash and I are both out of the hole, Monopoly money and jewels overflowing our pockets. "This scoundrel, who we thought was a man of civility —he's the notorious Captain Ash Coxswain, Pirate Tormenter of the Cold Celtic Sea. He's robbed from every soul on this ship."

Caius the Magistrate doesn't miss a beat. "It'll have to be a trial, then."

Caius is the best older brother imaginable.

It doesn't matter that he's leaving for medical school in Bristol in a couple of weeks; it doesn't matter that he's as tall as Justus and as magnificent as a Norse hero.

Despite everything that occupies him, Caius is clearheaded. He gets how important it is to address pirate offenses committed by eight-year-old boys.

"You going to make me walk the plank?" Ash asks him.

Caius takes a fistful of jewels from Ash's pocket and examines the evidence.

Some of the coins and rings have gone melty in the sun, and they stick to his fingers. "I have a much more fearsome fate in mind for you."

Ash twists in my clutches. "Cockle shards!"

I lead Ash to the deck, where Captain Justus can look on with his resolute eye, which always makes a sentencing feel more dire.

Caius stands on the steering deck before us. "For crimes committed against this sovereign ship, I hereby convict Johnny Minnow—hereafter to be known as Captain Ash Coxswain, Pirate Tormenter of the Cold Celtic Sea—to suffer a hindrance in the race from this ship, over that wild coast—whereon we'll shortly make landfall—to the gentle front porch of our beach house."

"Nooo!" cries Ash. "Mercy!"

"To a counting of fifteen shall you wait, Captain Ash," says Caius, "and if you still believe you can best Captain Corkscrew in a contest of speed—well, God be with you."

Caius steps down from the steering deck solemnly, his hand covering his heart.

Caius passes me on his way to the foremast, and I can't take my eyes off him.

He knows every inch of this ship and can command its sails as skillfully as Justus. Caius can read the weather by the feel of the wind, and he knows the sea's temper by its waves. Caius can navigate bodies of water and human bodies alike, and he knows the name of each one of my bones.

Caius visits the sails, easing their flashing and fastening them to their masts.

I pick up a length of rope, loose on the deck and give one end to Ash, which he grips with his towel-cuffed hands.

Together we knot it—or try to—like Caius is doing.

Ash watches Caius like I do, with awe in his eyes. Things are not happy for Ash at his home, and I'm glad that he's here and can share my big brother.

After a few moments, Caius has put all the sails to bed, and Captain Justus is steering the *Regulus* true to her berth.

We cut to the coast through a cacophony of frothy waves—waves splashing up spray and casting to us the tang of the sun-heated shallows, with their seaweed and salt-crusted reef tips and plankton and roe.

The second the *Regulus* touches her pier, I shout—"Landfall."

I strip the dishtowel handcuffs from Ash and tear over the length of the ship.

I leap the gap stretching between the bow and the beach, and despite the chiding from Empress Adara, I'm off, pounding the hardened sand and making for a woodland a hundred meters away.

Our beach house and its front porch—the finish line—rests just on the other side of its trees.

So many blue sky summer days, Ash and I have spent rambling among the oaks and junipers of this small woodland, reading Norse pirate histories and lost to the games of reliving them.

Though these cozy woods are nothing like the colossal Wentletrap Forest—glowering in the distance beyond the beach house, the trees in our small copse are magical-seeming, washed as they are with our tales.

Behind me on the ship, under the management of Caius the Magistrate, Captain Ash Coxswain is shouting off the count of his sentence.

I know he's after me when Empress Adara hollers, scolding him, too, for leaping the gap.

"Me lady," Ash calls. "The jewels I've robbed—they're for you."

And he means it. He admires my mum the way he regards Caius.

"My good man," Mum calls after him. "My hero."

I smile. Ash could use not just brothers, but a caring mum, too.

I glance over my shoulder and see that nothing remains of the mild Johnny Minnow. The boy streaming at me is all pirate—vicious in his determination to win.

The hindrance declared by Caius was a poor sentence for someone as athletic as Ash. Right at the edge of the woods, he moves past me.

But he doesn't leave me in the dust. Rather, he catches my hand and pulls me with him.

Ash is incredible—I can't believe he lets me be his best friend. In ecstasy, together, we fly among the gnarled trunks.

The trees rushing past are as familiar to us as our bodies. They're our trees. Or perhaps—we're they're boys.

I want to stay in our woodland, but Ash—gripping me—plows toward its western brink.

He's aiming, it seems, not for the beach house, but for the rocky coast.

At the edge of the woods, I have to stop and catch my breath.

I shake off Ash and linger inside the heavy musk of the trees, their close atmosphere wispy with mist.

I lean against a cradle made by a crooked, old oak that seems to keep not just me in the curve of its limbs, but my memories, too.

This oak—all these oaks—seem to hold in their heartwood the secrets and confessions and promises and discoveries that Ash and I have made in their company.

Sometimes it feels like these trees are immaterial.

Enchanted.

They seem more magnificent than mere plants, feeding on sunlight and sea mist as they do, holding such silence but for when storms rise, calling them to life, to dance, to roar.

Mostly, though, these trees feel like forever. They're old in their youth, and they'll be wiser yet when Ash and I vanish from the Earth. Every woodland we've played in—this small copse in Pembrokeshire, the ancient oak forest surrounding our houses in Devon, the dark Dartmoor Forest stretching south to the broad English Channel— their trees all seem to hold the recollection of our days in their glorious silence, in their scarred, mouthless faces.

I watch Ash race out of the woods and into a clearing—a stretch of packed sand entrenching the beach house and rippling to the west, ending in the crashing of waves.

There, on the plain between the woodland and the rocky coast, he waits for me, a clever smile lighting him—a knowing smile keeping his gratification that he can outrun me.

Ash is way more competitive than I am, better in every sport. And he's the most well-liked kid in school.

He makes sure that I know all this, that I regularly acknowledge how cool he is, which I'm glad to do. Because he calls me his best friend.

Few people at school look at me twice.

No one cares that I speak eight languages. Most think it's just odd. And the med school maths books that Caius loans me, to work from like puzzle books, get regularly swiped by kids who think they belong in the bin.

"You're not worn out, surely," shouts Ash. "Come on! Let's play at invisible swords on the dock."

I take off again, keeping the scent of the woods on my skin and adding to it the maritime brew of the open coastline—salty and fishy and windswept and cool.

Ash lets me catch up to him, and it's like we're two storm petrels soaring west, to the marvelous sea country that holds no memory but thrashes all knowledge of itself and all things in its path, clearing footprints and sandcastles, tearing to bits what memories—limbs of trees or wrecked ships, bottled messages, emptied shells, and stripped bones—are caught tumbling inside its strong current.

Ash pulls ahead of me, and I follow him in a hard run past the beach house, toward the rocky shore and down a wooden dock jetting into the ocean.

Ash stops at the dock's end, spins, and thrusts his rapier toward me.

I swipe away his strike as I shoot past, sending it poking into a dock post.

I have to bend against my knees to catch my breath, laughing as I am at Ash's clownish maneuvers to try and wrench his invisible rapier free from the post.

I point the tip of my own rapier straight at Ash's face. "Surrender, or you'll wear the mark of my blade on your mug for the whole ship to laugh at."

"Never!"

Ash, from playing at invisible swords earlier on the ship, already bears three marks on his face, inflicted with red ink.

He swipes his blade. "You give up, or I'll leave you with a pretty good scar for scaring the ladies."

"Swift," Mum calls. "Off the dock, please. If you and Ash want to play at invisible swords, come do it by the house. Let's have no spills into the water."

"I don't care a heap of sardines for the ladies." I lunge.

A tap with a finger means a rapier strike and entitles the aggressor to scrawl a mark on the victim.

I do. Right across Ash's cheek. It looks real. Bloody.

Ash, clutching his chest, sinks to his knees. "This wound's mortal!"

"No it isn't." I back up. "I just clipped your cheek."

"Well, say that you didn't." Ash gets to his feet. "Say you plunged it home in my chest or my belly. Say you did. That'd be a mortal wound and much more interesting."

"All right." I take my stance and thrust the rapier straight to his chest.

Home goes the blade. Ash sprawls on the dock and drops into a fit of theatrical twitching.

"Come off the dock, lads," hollers Caius.

Mum follows Caius, the two of them carrying sailing supplies up the path leading to the beach house. "Now, Swift!"

"Be right there." Holding my marker cocked, I kneel over Ash. "I just have to finish off this pirate rascal."

"Make it quick," comes Mum's irritated voice, from the house's front porch.

I apply a line of red jagged ink across Ash's chest, at the left intercostal space where Caius says the heart beats its strongest.

One mighty last twitch—and—

Ash is gone.

Dead as a driftwood plank.

Ash pushes to his elbows. "Bet you can't get me again."

I glance toward the beach house.

Mum and Caius aren't there. Neither is Justus. They must've all gone inside.

They want us up by the house, but—invisible swords is far better played with a backdrop of water.

I narrow my eyes at Ash. "Bet I can."

And I certainly can. In a meeting of rapiers, I almost always prevail. It's about the only thing at which Ash ever allows me to win, making each victory honey sweet.

"Your blade won't so much as come near me," says Ash with gusto. "But look how mine bites!" He runs at me.

I ease aside, sending Ash tumbling to his knees on the dock. "Yours bites, does it? Seems tame as a tuna fish to me."

Ash clambers to his feet and rushes me.

A smart flick does the job, and Ash stumbles once again, gripping his ribs where a rapier handle would be sticking out.

Sometimes it feels like this game of swordplay—Ash perpetually losing—is his bid to keep me, tiring of always trailing behind, from shaking him off.

But how could I shake him off? I call Ash my best friend, too.

I can beat Ash in any subject at school, though. I can beat anyone. But on that score, Ash refuses to compete.

"I'm finished," Ash whispers, barely managing to make it back up to his feet. "You're witness to the last words of Captain Ash Coxswain, Pirate Tormentor of the Cold Celtic Sea."

I salute.

Ash spins on a heel and falls backwards.

A glorious, tragic fall it would've been, had his aim been on point toward the dock. But he falls right off its edge and splashes into the water.

I rush to the dock's edge. "Ash?"

Nothing.

I wait.

If this is a trick, Ash will have to come up in a second.

"Ash?"

Bubbles. Some rippling. And then—steady waves.

Ash isn't coming up.

Ash is drowning.

"Mum!" I call toward the house. "Father!"

No one comes out of the house.

I start to run to it but stop. I stare at the dark, rocking water. Ash is down there.

I crash to my knees on the dock.

I've been trained to help struggling swimmers. Well, not trained, exactly, but I've seen it. Well, not directly, but online. And Caius has done it and told me about it.

"Mum," I scream. "Father! Caius!"

I could dive, but—Caius once told me that in water accidents, the rescuer often drowns, too.

Kneeling on the dock before the sloshing current, I can comprehend why.

The water is turbulent and deep here, where the dock meets the shore rocks. Plus, it's cold. Ice cold.

I look back toward the beach house.

There's no one in sight.

No one's coming.

I strip off my trousers and kick off my shoes. I fill my lungs with possibly all the coastal air in Wales. I dive.

Down I sink, my body convulsing with the agony of cold water. I pull down to where the light thins. Down into worlds removed from air. Down towards where a pale hand drifts beside a dark head.

The burning in my lungs begins well before I can reach Ash where he hangs.

I must let go of bubbles—precious oxygen bubbles—to keep from sucking down seawater.

My eyes sting. My heart deafens.

I struggle down, down to the eerie weeds swaying darkly on the seafloor.

I catch Ash's hand. His body is a deadweight as I drag him up from the murk.

Holding Ash—limp—to my chest, I kick hard. I let out more bubbles. Break the water's surface. I suck a deep breath while shadows clear from my eyes.

Ash doesn't breathe. His eyelids stay closed.

I kick toward the shore.

But the current is a fist dragging us back.

Already, we're a dozen feet from the shore rocks, and the breakers aren't giving us any chance at reaching them.

Don't panic. Float. Keep parallel to the coast. Don't try to swim to it—that's a losing fight.

I breathe as steadily as I can between waves. I kick, keeping parallel to the coast. I glance around for anything to grab, but there's nothing. Ash's cold body, rubbery, is the only thing nearby to grip, and as strongly as I'm trying to keep us both afloat, his weight is dragging me down.

I struggle to think.

Swim parallel to the coast. That's all I know about surviving a fall into the sea. I've many times imagined falling in, but never with my best friend—not breathing—in tow.

A tall wave curls over us, dousing our faces.

I heave Ash higher, resting the back of his head on my shoulder.

Ash coughs up water. Breathes. Cries out.

Arms grasping. Legs kicking.

I can barely keep hold of him.

"Ash, stop." I manage a tighter grip. "Calm down. I have you. Keep breathing."

"Who has you?" Ash rasps.

I think fast. "The kraken. Its tentacles are holding us up."

Ash seems to be picturing it. He lets off with trying to wrap his arms around my head.

"Don't move, okay?" I say. "Not a muscle. Trust me."

"I want my father." Ash is crying. "You let me fall. Why'd you let me fall in?"

The water spins us away from the rocky shore and carries us north of the beach house.

I've been in water this cold before, but never without a wetsuit. After just these few minutes, my legs are tending numb.

Mum comes into view. "Swift?" She scans the dock, the edge of the rocks. "Ash?"

"Mum," I shout. 'Help' would've been next, but I swallow a mouthful of water.

Mum screams. She races over a stretch of sandy land to the rocky sea wall.

Running along the waterline, she seems faster than the current, but barely, and by the time she reaches the end of the shore rocks, Ash and I are spinning toward the open ocean.

The open ocean. Where jellyfish and water snakes drift. Where sharks swim.

I can't help my breathing going manic.

I twist us to facing the coast. I stare at Mum—running along the shallows and not keeping up.

"Let go," says Ash. "I can swim."

Ash probably can't swim. Or not well, after what happened to him. And apart, the current might carry us each faster. Or me this way and Ash that.

Mum might be able to reach one of us, but not both.

We have to stay together.

Water smashes into us.

"Let go of me." Ash squirms.

A wave buries us.

Up we come, me gripping Ash's shoulders with arms I can't feel.

Ash fights to get free. Claws my arms. Kicks. Swipes at my face.

Even if I wanted to, though, I couldn't let go of him. My arms are frozen, contracted around Ash's shoulders.

"You're killing me," says Ash.

I kick as hard as I can to stay over the waves. "Hey—what's that?"

Ash stills.

"In the sky," I say. "There. What is that?"

"Where?"

The current twists us to face the open ocean.

"The clouds," I say. "Look at those clouds."

"There aren't any clouds."

"One coming from the north is shaped just like a pirate ship. See it?"

"Where?"

Heavy hands grip us and cast us onto a body board.

"Hang on, lads, tight as you can." It's my father. Justus.

He sees our hands fixed on the board, then kicks hard, ferrying us to the shore.

2

A wave heaves the body board against the rocks.

My head strikes. Caius catches me by an arm and a leg and drags me out of the water.

Mum's pulling out Ash and helping Justus climb onto the rocks. She cradles Ash like he's her own boy.

I'm relieved that Ash is out of the water, and that it's Mum who has him. Ash needs a mum, now more than ever. But his mum won't be coming.

Caius is speaking to me, but I can't respond. Not because I'm injured too badly or breathed too much seawater—but because I can't take my eyes off Ash. He's just lying in Mum's arms. What if he isn't all right?

But after a moment, he seems all right. Justus is helping him cough up more water. Soon, Ash is breathing and moving—crying with Mum.

Mum untangles a wool throw from a heap of blankets they brought out and wraps Ash.

"You'll be fine, lad." Justus blots tears off Ash's face. "Your father is on his way."

"Swift." Caius cradles my cheek and makes me look at him. "Answer me. Does breathing hurt?"

I realize he's holding a cloth to my head, and when he pulls it away, I see blood on it.

Caius unfolds another wool blanket and lays me down on it.

"Breathing doesn't hurt," I tell him. "Is my head split open?" I try to feel it, but Caius keeps my hand down.

"How much water did you swallow? Did you choke?" He feels of my chest and neck. Listens to me breathe. Examines my eyes. Checks the cut on my head.

"I swallowed a lot of water," I say. "I don't think I breathed much of it."

"Swift seems all right," Caius tells Mum and Justus. He glances at Ash. "How long until the air ambulance arrives?"

Justus scans the sky. "Any minute." He kneels over Ash and smiles reassuringly. "The air ambulance is just a precaution."

It's hard to tell whether Ash is really all right. He seems not able to look at me.

"Why'd you two have to go and tumble off the dock?" Caius strips off his flannel overshirt. He pulls the blanket away from my shoulders and wraps me in the flannel, warm from his body. He again bundles the blanket around me. "How many times have we told you not to play by the water alone? How many times did we call you to come off the dock? Not listening is how lads tumble into the sea."

"I didn't tumble," I say. "Ash did."

Caius' expression shifts from terror-stricken to something like surprise.

Justus watches me with an appraising look. Mum's eyes on me are full of fear.

"Swift…" Justus seems at a loss for words. "My lad…"

"I want my father," says Ash, from within his cocoon of wool blanket.

Mum wraps her arm around Ash. "It'll be a bit warmer up by the porch. Would you like to come with me and wait for your father there?"

Caius guides me to sitting up.

"Ash." I try to catch his glance, but he offers me nothing. "Are you okay?"

Though he won't speak to me, Ash is standing up on his own now.

He's holding Mum's hand as they walk to the beach house.

"Why does he seem so out of it?" I ask Caius.

"I'm sure he'll be all right," says Caius. "I'd like you not to worry about him." He settles beside me and wraps his arm around my shoulders. "So—you dove into the water after him? Or, what happened?"

I can't really process what happened. I can only stare at Ash, sitting on the front porch with Mum now, Justus standing alongside.

"Ash fell in, right?" Caius catches my glance. "Is that how it went? Then—you dove?"

"Deep," I say. "To where the water was black."

Caius holds his warm hand against my chest. He tightens the blanket around my shoulders.

Guarded by him like this, I can no longer see Ash.

"Are you angry with me?" I rest my gaze on Caius. "I should've brought him off the dock."

"You've got that right." Caius glances beneath the cloth on my head. "But no, I'm not angry. I'm just relieved—still a little bit scared. Are you?"

"I thought I was going to die." I move the blanket away from my face and watch Ash. "I thought Ash had drowned."

Caius glances back at the others. "Mum is certainly wanting you beside her. Do you think you can walk?"

I let him help me to my feet.

Caius guides me along the path leading to the beach house.

When we reach the front porch, I stand before Mum and Ash. Mum draws me to her and holds me closely by her side.

Ash stands away from us and walks off.

"Ash?" I call after him. "Can you please say if you're all right?"

He trudges to the middle of the sandy yard and sits down by himself.

Caius settles closely beside me as though protecting me; as though worried that even from here I might tumble into the water.

Justus examines me the way Caius did.

He seems satisfied by the assessment and glances at Adara, at Caius. "The air ambulance should arrive soon."

Justus follows to where Ash has retreated and kneels by him. He wraps a second blanket around Ash, which Ash seems grateful for, though he's still refusing to look at anyone.

Ash's father, Mr. Emberly, pulls in.

He trips out of his car and races across the sandy stretch. He drops to his knees before Ash and wraps him in his arms.

The way Justus is holding onto Mr. Emberly's shoulder, it seems Mr. Emberly is crying.

Mr. Emberly speaks to Justus a moment, both of them glancing at me.

Mr. Emberly stands away from Ash and approaches the porch.

With Ash seeming upset with me, with Caius and the others assuming, at first, that we both fell in—maybe that I was responsible for Ash falling in—Mr. Emberly might think the same thing.

My ears ring with echoes of Mum and Caius calling us to come off the dock.

I lean into Caius and brace for Mr. Emberly to lay into me.

But he doesn't.

He pulls me into a hug, then holds me away from him. "You rescued my lad. I don't know what to say, except—thank you."

I can't accept those thanks. I didn't earn them. I didn't lead Ash off the dock.

And I'm still shaky from the fear of the open ocean, from straining to swim for so long. I'm warming underneath Caius' flannel and the blanket he's got me wrapped in—but even so, I can't manage any real grip on myself. All I can do is sit in silence before Mr. Emberly.

Ash, still on the lawn with Justus, finally looks back at me.

Our gazes catch.

Ash's expression offers me no solace, though. It seems like terror, at first—but, after studying him a moment, I can read that it isn't. This isn't any shade of fear.

It's hate.

Ash can cast the most interesting expressions, and I know this one well. His face is handsome, and the range of looks he can conjure always has drawn me. Even this one is somehow charming, though it's savage, and I can't look away from it.

This is the look he's used on other kids at school. Kids he wants nothing to do with. It's an expression that's always brought me comfort because it marks me as someone welcome in his company, while others are excluded.

Now, though, his hate is directed at me.

The feel of it, I can't bear. I feel cast out. And Ash seems to be growing even angrier. He seems not to like his father gazing on me.

Could Ash—my best friend—really shake me off so suddenly? The pain of the possibility lashes like a shock of cold water.

"I'm sorry." I glance up at Mr. Emberly. "Tell Ash I'm sorry."

"My dear lad, you have nothing to be sorry for," says Mr. Emberly.

Ash clearly received his expressiveness from his father, and it's some relief to feel so surely that Mr. Emberly isn't upset with me. But I wish Ash would come around.

"Ash is just frightened at the moment," says Mr. Emberly. "I imagine you are, too."

"Ash won't speak to me," I say.

Mr. Emberly crouches before me, so we're eye to eye. "His mum just left us, you know. He's taken to blaming other people when no wrongdoing has happened. It's just his way of dealing with that sorrow. I'm sure he'll come around if you're patient. Can you be patient for him?"

Of course I can. I nod.

Mr. Emberly stands as the blades of an air ambulance cut the sky.

3

I wander into the ancient forest—what Ash and I call our "Oak Empire," inside of which our two houses in Devon are nestled.

It's been three weeks since The Tumble, and Ash hasn't spoken a word to me at school. He hasn't so much as looked at me.

But I'm not going to let The Tumble destroy what we have. Ash is like a brother—I can't let go of that.

Mr. Emberly asked me to be patient with Ash, which I can be. But Ash has to meet me at least some of the way. He's got to listen to what I have to say.

And it's time for us to get past this. Our birthdays are the same week, and they're coming up. We're about to turn nine, and we always celebrate our birthdays together. Surely, he'll want to.

And maybe he does, because there he is, sitting against his favorite climbing oak, with his rucksack beside him, comic books spilling out of it.

He wouldn't have come out here, to Oak Empire, to that specific tree that I know he loves, if he didn't want me to find him.

I approach.

Though he must hear me coming, must see me out of the corner of his eye, he isn't looking up.

"Ash." I stop before him.

He turns the page of his comic.

"I've been wondering how you are." I crouch down and look at him, at eye level.

Keeping his gaze on his comic, he says, "Please leave me alone."

"Why have you been ignoring me?"

He glances at me, his eyes darkly glinting with the hatred that marred his expression before. "Because you're not safe."

I stand. "What do you mean?"

Ash gathers his comics into his rucksack in a flustered way.

I back off.

"This tree is on my side of the property line," says Ash. "You stay on your side of the line, and I'll stay on mine. If you cross over, I'll tell my father, and you'll get in big trouble."

I glance up and down the woodland, wondering how he could call any part of it "yours" or "mine." The forest seems inviting, on all fronts.

And every tree seems to be quietly holding our memories still, keeping them folded like unborn leaves, waiting for a day to dawn when the strengthening sunlight might call them to again sail in the wind.

"Our birthdays, though," I say. "Don't you want to celebrate together?"

"Why would I want a birthday party with you?" Ash stands. Shoulders his rucksack. "I almost died because of you." He hauls off.

"I know you were scared—so was I," I call after him. "But we're all right."

Ash is jogging now, like he's hurrying to where he'll be out of earshot.

"Don't you miss me?" I call after him.

Ash stops. Bends down. He picks up a stone and comes toward me a few paces. He winds back his arm and casts the stone.

I can't believe what I'm seeing. I don't flinch, don't dodge.

The stone hits me square on the cheek.

I watch it tumble to the ground. I can't breathe as I stare up at Ash.

"I said—leave me alone." Ash breaks into a run and disappears into the brush.

4

Caius holds a plastic bag of ice in a towel to my face. "You're done trying to make friends again with him, all right?"

How can I agree to that? Ash and me—our friendship feels eternal.

I take the icepack into my own hand and lean against the back of my kitchen chair.

"Look, when a kid loses his mum like Ash has," says Caius, "it messes with him pretty bad. Think what it would be like if Mum were to walk out, then refuse to see any of us."

I can't even imagine it. Mum, too, seems eternal.

"That's why I want to mend things," I tell Caius, my voice shaky.

He watches me closely. "You're still having a tough time getting your bearings, aren't you?"

Of course I'm having a tough time getting my bearings. My best friend just hurt me. On purpose.

A thickness weighs in my chest, like a sort of grief that won't let go of my heart but spurs it to race. And I still feel incapable of drawing whole breaths—the only way to get enough air is to take it in quick gasps.

Caius taps the pulse in my neck as he watches me breathe. "I think this is panicking." He stands and takes off his flannel overshirt. He wraps it around me. He leans on the table and watches me closely.

After a moment of feeling him so near, of smelling the warmth of his shirt, of watching his eyes resting on mine and not threatening to focus elsewhere, breathing grows easier.

"Mr. Emberly said to be patient with Ash," I tell Caius. "I was patient for three weeks. How much longer can he make me wait?"

"I know you want to help Ash." Caius eases again to sitting. "But it seems you can't. Friendships must go both ways. If he's pushing you off, then I'm sorry, but that's probably the end of things."

I can't accept that. Not ever. Friendships, like forests, seem eternal. Even the phrase "Swift and Ash" seems to have grown into a single word—the way two trees closely planted might intertwine with each other.

And the trees in Oak Empire and in Dartmoor and in Pembrokeshire keep our memories, still.

I can imagine slipping into Oak Empire, with Ash, fifty years from now and still feeling how we belong to its trees. Trees with rotted-out holes that've hidden our treasures; trees with trunks knotty enough and limbs twisty enough for climbing races, for hanging from and falling out of, for reading, for doing nothing but witnessing the sky turning marigold, for holding two best friends watching the night swiftly falling, to see the stars strengthening to light a tree's crown.

Caius brings my hand, along with the ice pack, away from my face and studies the bruise.

"Why'd his mum have to leave him in the first place?" I ask.

"People do all kinds of crazy things when they're unhappy," says Caius. "I heard Mr. Emberly telling Justus that it was for the best, sad as it is. You've probably seen how often she raised her voice at Ash. It seems she had some troubles of her own. With drugs, maybe. With alcohol certainly. I'm sure Ash is mortified by how she behaved. But don't you go spreading that around school. Ash wouldn't thank you for that. I'm only talking it over with you so you'll understand."

"I already knew what his mum was like," I say. "And of course I never talk about her at school. What I don't get is—if Ash is so unhappy, why won't he let me help him?"

"Here's a hard truth," said Caius. "You ready?"

I watch him.

"You can't control other people. Even if you think you know what's best for someone, you can't dictate what they do."

"That doesn't seem right," I say. "You and Justus and Mum dictate plenty to me about what I should do."

Caius casts me a look. "That's different. We're raising you. What I mean is—you can't control Ash. And you shouldn't let him control you."

It still doesn't seem right. If I know that Ash needs my friendship, then letting him refuse it seems unloving.

And anyway, Ash has always, to some extent, controlled me. It's been our way. He tells me what to do, and I usually do it. Nothing seems very wrong with that. It's been fun, actually. And it's kept Ash close.

"If Ash told me to do something right now," I say, "I'd do it. Gladly."

Caius casts me a judgy sort of look.

He's seen the way Ash and I play. He's never liked the way Ash "bosses me around."

Bossy or not, though, these weeks without Ash have been desolate. No one else at school cares about me. And I still can't fully make sense of The Tumble. Even now, I can't recall it but in just flashes. Who could possibly understand that besides Ash?

And this punishment that Ash is dealing me seems to be taking hold in a deep way. It's like his hateful expression lobbed a rock at my heart that sank in.

"You don't get it," I tell Caius. "Ash can be so much fun when I do what he tells me."

"Ash might be fun." Caius snips a small butterfly bandage. "So much fun, in fact, that you'll do the next crazy thing, and the next." He lays the bandage carefully over a small cut that the stone opened on my cheek.

"Do you blame Ash for The Tumble?" I ask.

"I don't blame either one of you. But it was his responsibility, as well as yours, to heed us. You both heard us calling. And you both are smart enough to have realized that what you were doing was dangerous—playing by the water with no one around."

I feel of my cheek, buttoned up by my brother.

"I want Ash to be like you," I tell him. "Eternal."

"That lad is no brother to you," says Caius. "And this is the nature of life. Change. You're going to have to learn to brave that."

He fixes his gaze on me. "As seriously as I warned you to get off the dock, I'm warning you now that you have to let go of him."

He traces the healing scar on my forehead from its strike on the rocks before he pulled me out of the water.

"This is two cuts, now, Ash has laid on my brother. I promise you, I won't handle it well if you come home with another."

"Will you promise to be nice to him, though, if you see him?" I ask. "If he senses that someone around here doesn't like him, it'll just drive him further away?"

Caius takes the ice pack from my hand. "I don't think I'll run into the lad, and that pleases me." He goes to the sink and dumps the ice and melt water down the drain. "But if I do, I'll be civil—I promise." He glances up. "And what promise can you make me?"

"I'll try to leave him be," I say. "But if he comes back wanting to mend things, I'm letting him."

"So loyal a friend." Caius shakes his head. "Ash doesn't realize how lucky he is."

5

Staying away from Ash's side of Oak Empire is difficult.

I'm learning to be in these yellowing woods on my own, but it isn't easy. It seems death ranks the air, coating our memories, heavy in the trees, with the sorrow that would've fallen if Ash had died on the day of The Tumble.

I mostly read out here. Norse mythology and poetry, in Old Norse. Some in Icelandic.

The book I'm reading now—*The Star of Atlantis*—is on sea legends and pirate fantasies. I found it in an old bookshop in Exeter, in a box covered in cobwebs. I have other maritime history and myth books like this, and reading them was something Ash and I often did together.

Ash didn't know anything about Welsh and Icelandic piracy, about the legends of sea monsters and the history of Celtic seafaring, until I introduced him to it. Most of my books, Ash still has.

The tree that I'm leaning against will soon hold a treehouse. Caius and I are building it together. It's his final gift to me, he says, before he's off to Bristol to get lost in his medical studies.

I can't quite believe Caius really is leaving. I feel like I somehow should stop those wheels turning—it's the same need that presses me to want to make Ash forgive me.

But I can't control either of them. This is the nature of life, Caius said. Change.

A crack of a twig in the forest summons my gaze from my book.

Walking in the golden distance, watching me through a web of barren branches, is Ash.

He's approaching slowly, cautiously, it seems. And he's carrying what looks like a pillowcase, heavy with some sort of load.

When we played here together, we each would bring a pillowcase full of toys.

I close my book. Stand.

Seeing him moving through the evening mists of the woodland is medicine.

In the orange and marigold and pale green of the forest, with its rare shafts of copper light streaming from the setting sun, Ash looks dappled like he himself is one of the trees.

Just as ancient.

As full of memory.

Permanent.

The heaviness in my heart seems to melt.

"I've been waiting for you to come out here," shouts Ash, from a good distance away.

But he's closing that distance.

"I've been hoping to see you, too," I call. "Listen, I know you've been upset with me, with your Mum, but I'd like you to know——"

"There's no point in saying whatever you're getting at." Ash stops a few meters in front of me.

His face looks cold, despite that the late summer evening is still grasping a bit of the day's warmth.

There's a paleness in his cheeks; an emptiness in his eyes.

He isn't the Ash of the clever expressions, of the adventurous games. He isn't the Ash that would lead me to laughing 'til I couldn't stand. He seems altogether changed.

But he's come.

And surely, he's got something great in that pillowcase. As much as I've missed him, he has to have missed me a little.

"I've got a new sea legend book." I show him *The Star of Atlantis*. "It's about the lost treasure we've read about——hidden someplace in Wales. I was just thinking about how much fun it would be to read this with you. It says more about the treasure——the Star of Atlantis—— than any other book I've seen."

Ash glances at it. "Is it written in English?"

"Mostly," I say. "The top of each page holds odd characters that I can't make out. But I'm going to study them. If it's some dialect of Old Norse, I can probably translate it for you."

"Translate it, so—what? You can rub in how much smarter you are than me?"

I try moving toward him, but he takes a step back.

I stop. "I don't think I'm smarter than you. The games you come up with—they're brilliant."

Ash seems to be growing furious. "You say that, and yet you wanted me trapped under the cold water."

"You do realize I jumped into that cold water after you, right?"

"Right," says Ash. "Another one of ten thousand moments when you outdid me."

"You think there was some kind of competition going on when you fell in the water?" I ask. "That doesn't make any sense."

But it sort of does make sense, knowing Ash. In his mind, everything's a contest.

It dawns on me how I might approach this.

"Do you wish that I'd fallen off the dock, and that you were the one to rescue me?" I ask. "Do you think that by pulling you up from the deep water, I'm some kind of hero? Because I'll tell you right now —I'm not. I should've listened to Mum and Caius when they asked us to come away."

"Yeah, you should've." Ash spat the words. "You're saying that you aren't a hero, but I know you think you are. You must be loving this. It's why you let me fall in the first place."

"Ash—"

"You're always trying to get one up on me, and you finally did, and now you've won—"

"Hey, calm down—"

"I hope you're happy that you're finally on top—that you've managed to win, even though you almost killed someone."

"Stop it!"

He teeters back.

So do I. I didn't mean to yell at him.

He must think I meant some cruelty by it, though. His eyes are tearing.

We both know his mum yelled at him like that. We've both been afraid of her.

I glance down. "I didn't mean to yell. I just needed you to stop."

Ash marches forward and dumps the contents of the pillowcase at my feet.

Play money. Candy jewels. Plastic gemstones and pearls. Norse mythology action figures. Toy swords. Plastic sailing ships and a couple of wooden ones—models—that we glued together. Models now splintering upon hitting the ground.

"All this junk is yours," says Ash. "I don't want it."

Water flashes into my eyes at how final this feels. It's like, in this moment, the piece of Ash that's grown into me is being extracted.

"Keep away from me." Ash backs up.

"Hold on." I start to follow, but he sets into a run.

I run after him. "These aren't all my things." I glance back at the pile of what amounts to plastic and rubbish. "What about my antique books? You've got all of them."

"I have not," he shouts back.

But he certainly has. More than twenty, in fact, that I've collected over the last few years.

Ocean mythology books. Norse legends. Welsh histories of coastal clans that thrived in the glory days of Celtic Sea piracy.

I stop and yell—"Don't take my books."

Way ahead of me, he turns. "So you're calling me a thief? A liar?"

"That's not what I'm doing. I want you and the books."

"You don't care about me," Ash shouts. "When I fell, you could've caught me. But you didn't, so you could come out the hero. And now you're saying I've stolen from you so you can keep your foot on my neck. You'll probably spread all around school that my mum left and why."

"Ash—I won't tell anyone. Anything."

"You want to help me?" He seems to smile as he turns away. "Stay away from me. Forever."

"Ash—" I shout.

But he's disappearing into the mist, and it's clear that following him would be pointless.

So I just watch him vanish.

I return to my tree, to the pile of junk at its base.

I cradle my book. *The Star of Atlantis*. My only sea legend book remaining.

I feel of its pages. Trace the silver Celtic star on its cover.

In a way, I'm glad my books are at Ash's house. Through them, a piece of me remains with him. Maybe, in keeping them, he'll realize that he wants me close.

I watch the vapor of the falling night twist, as though by some miracle of the gray twilight, Ash, like a lighting star, will loom out of it.

But of course he doesn't.

I lean against my tree and hold my book tight to my chest where it feels like a wound has been laid. My heart beating against the book is manic, the way it felt in the depths of the ocean. Caius called the effect "panic" and coached me on how to calm down, how to still myself.

I focus on the beating of my heart, like he said. I draw slow breaths, like a steady wind, and visualize the air cooling me from the inside out, like a storm wind refreshing a piping beach.

But my heart now seems lit by a fire that can't be quenched.

I kneel before the tree and shove all the cheap treasure into a split near its base where the heartwood is rotted.

I nestle against the tree, willing myself to reach some kind of stasis.

This feeling of falling, of desolation—this must be the feeling of change.

Caius said I'll have to learn to brave this.

But confronting it, I can't seem to grasp enough air. It's like I'm underneath a cold current, struggling, trying to surface, and failing.

6

Oak Empire, around me, grows dark. The mist has moved in and is thick as a blanket, muting the distant lights glinting from the windows of my house.

I should go in soon. If I'm out too long past dark, my family will worry.

But I want to stay in the forest. My fingers, clenching the soil, might perhaps siphon—as by roots—the past the trees hold.

A sound rings—a cry.

I startle to standing.

I slide my book into my rucksack.

"Hello?" I call, my voice unsteady.

I shoulder my rucksack.

The cry sounds again.

It's something between a whine and a scream. All at once canine and human.

I feel my way through the dark woods, tree by tree, my hands finding familiar trunks and limbs.

The edges of the forest are higher than its center, like a moon crater.

Just beyond the threshold of higher, thick trees, the mist disperses into less a cloud bank and more a veil. There, in the clearing beyond the woodland, moonlight traces the shadows of thinned trees.

As I climb out of the wood's edge, I see it.

In a small, open glade, clear of mist, lies a fox.

It sees me. It smells me. It rises to its feet.

But it again drops to lying down.

Even at this distance, I can see that its leg is mangled. It looks like it's been wounded for some time—the blood on it isn't fresh, but coagulated and dark.

I hold up my hands, hoping the fox might read the gesture as peaceful. "What have you been through?" I step closer.

The whine shifts to a low growl.

I kneel. "It's okay."

At the sight of an animal in pain, my stomach feels punched. My legs ache. Maybe the fox got into a fight and lost. Maybe he stepped in a trap and won freedom only long enough for an infection to set in.

If I can just get him to trust me a little, I could carry him home. Caius and Justus would know what to make of that leg, and we could get him to a vet.

But even as plans of how I might approach him course through my mind, even as I'm pulling off my hoodie and making out of it a sort of carrying satchel that could keep him warm, I realize my efforts will be wasted.

The fox seems too weak to hold up his head for more than a second. And his breathing is shallow. It's almost undetectable.

The fox is certainly close to death.

Watching him—a fellow being in terrible pain and unable to receive comfort, knowing I can do nothing—something inside my chest seems to break.

The world is all of change. And it's ridden with loss. It's the way of things, says Caius.

But how not to lose oneself? How not to lose those you love in the face of unstoppable pain?

I again try to approach, and the fox allows it, somewhat.

His eyes fix on me, and he pins his ears to his skull. He rumbles a low growl that seems to warn—injured leg or not, death coming or not, he will bite if I press him.

"It's all right." A meter from him, I sit. "You're not alone. I'm here with you. I'll stay."

The fox seems to take some comfort in seeing that I've stopped advancing.

I pull a bottle of water from my rucksack.

I've got no food, but that probably doesn't matter. In his state, he wouldn't eat. But even a creature close to death might respond to the instinct of thirst.

I reach to pour water in front of him. "Here."

A flash of teeth in the moonlight. A snarl that rakes my ears.

I've jumped back before I realized I needed to move.

I glance down at myself—look for blood from a bite wound.

Nothing hurts. There's no blood. He didn't catch my skin or clothes with those sharp teeth.

He eyes me a few moments—long enough to seem convinced that I'll remain still.

He pulls himself to the water puddle. He drinks.

I sit back down. Slowly.

I'm still close to him, but I'm beyond what seems to be his strike range.

He watches me but doesn't leave the water.

After a moment, he lays down by the puddle, his snout partway in it. He laps at the earth.

"You're not alone," I tell the fox. "Things change, but I'll make sure that you're not alone."

I hate the sound of the words as I speak them. It hurts to admit that life keeps unfolding, on the far side of change. In this moment, a clean ending seems easier than change.

But perhaps beyond change, beyond a treacherous severing of a friendship; beyond a loss of a brother who's as good as a father; beyond a near death; beyond a mum leaving—a boy might find himself still not alone.

That place, though, is dark. I haven't a clue whether I may be right.

Every breath the fox draws is a whine, and its sound stings in my chest.

But something about bearing this—something about being here in this dark hour with him—it seems also to lay a stitch over the pain that Ash punched there.

The fox looks at me with an expression of intelligence. It's like he has stories to tell; like he's kept a treasure of memories, alongside these trees.

"What kind of life did you have in Oak Empire?" My voice seems to be of some comfort to the fox. His ears stand tall again.

"Are you an old fox?" I ask, serving him words—all the medicine I've got. "How old are you, I wonder?"

He quirks an ear, and his whining stops.

I slowly pull my book from my rucksack.

"What if you're a very old fox? An ancient fox, like this forest. What if you're old enough to know of the Icelandic pirates who sailed the Celtic Sea, in olden times? They've hidden a marvelous treasure. Maybe you know that."

I hold before him *The Star of Atlantis*.

"It's a treasure that's said to be still out there someplace."

All this, I wanted to talk over with Ash. This is the excitement I wanted to share with him, over my new book.

Ash loves all my books. Clearly—he's kept them. But none of the books we've love are like this one. The others seem like planetary spheres, winging, while this book—*The Star of Atlantis*—is like a sun. The center of Celtic Sea myths.

"Would you like to hear the way to an actual Welsh treasure?" I ask the fox.

He looks at me as though he would like to hear.

I slide a flashlight from my rucksack, which he allows. I train its beam on the page of my book, where I left off when Ash discovered me.

When the shore draws long and straight, skim the briny banks. Be swallowed by Sterncastle Cove. Seek the islet, round as Earth, studded with Kraken fangs.

Mind the deeps for mermaid tails, shimmering blue and green. Heed their song, but touch the water not, lest your life be forfeit to their goddess.

Always keep a weather eye on the mist coiling in the cove, for through it paddles old Grog Blossom, always dead, yet ever awake, cursed to forever sail as watchman over the Star of Atlantis.

The fox listens carefully to the words, though he seems unable to make out their meaning any better than I can.

"It's cryptic, I know." I feed the book back into my rucksack.

The fox rests his head on the ground. He lets a gentle whine.

I clench my hoodie, wanting to just snap him up and bind him and carry him home.

But how that would shock him. The fury of the struggle itself might kill him. And he'd certainly mangle me for terrifying him so.

I meet his small eyes. "I wish I could stop this."

The fox seems to know that I want to. I find comfort in imagining that perhaps he even knows that I can't.

He claws the ground, pulling himself nearer.

I freeze. Is he trying to chase me off? Is this an instinct awakening, perceiving anything before him as a threat? Will he displace his aggression from the pain, from his fear, in an attack?

I hold myself stone still. It seems any sudden move might provoke him to bite.

His whining persists, issuing from between sharp teeth, clenched.

I can't move away without risking alarming him. All I can do is slowly lift my hands to my chest, preparing to guard my face, at least, should he strike.

He reaches me.

His claws, sharp as branch tips, graze my leg.

I hold my breath and am mindful of nothing but the slam of my heart as he pulls himself close enough to bite. He needs only open his jaws.

But he doesn't.

He rests his cheek on my thigh.

A long whine drifts from him like a mist trailing from the woods to the sea.

He lies motionless, his eyes no longer blinking. Perhaps no longer seeing.

He stops breathing.

I'm too petrified by his stillness to think. All I can do is watch tears slip off my chin and dampen his fur.

I hold steady for a few minutes, until I'm certain he's passed; longer than it seemed I was under the water with Ash.

And then I gather him into my arms.

He's lighter than he looks. Probably, he's emaciated from that injury.

I hold him to my chest, saturating my clothes, my skin with his musk, wholly wild.

There's a beauty about the stillness of the fox that surprises me.

His tail is broad and handsome. The mottling of his fur, artistic. His dilated eyes have captured the night canopy in its boundlessness.

And there's a deeper loveliness striking me yet. It's a humbling sense of gratitude that I—worthless to the fox in his distress—still found a place of belonging in this, his final night.

A sense of peace hangs in the silence around us, the gentle wind no longer carrying his cry.

This is the fox's peace. There was no part for me to play at his passing but to simply be present with him.

And now that he's gone, now that I'm wholly cut loose from him, I see that my part is to simply move forward. To go further into the night.

"I'm sorry, though," I whisper. "You seem to have gone to a place where there isn't any light."

7

Voices are calling in the forest. Voices belonging to Caius and Justus. Voices shouting my name.

I try to respond, but tears choke me.

"He's there," shouts Caius.

Soon, two light beams are on me, but I can't call out any response to Justus and Caius, rushing up the forest slope toward this glade. I can't even really look up.

I only can cradle the fox.

Caius kneels ever so gently in front of me and the fox.

He seems confounded, like he's struggling to make out what he's seeing. He seems to be trying to measure whether the fox is a danger to us. Whether I'm bitten.

"He's gone," I manage.

Justus and Caius glance at one another. Justus seems to impart some gesture that Caius catches, though I can't focus well enough on them to read it.

Caius reaches for the body of the fox and slips him from my arms. He hands the limp animal to Justus, who disappears with it into the forest.

"Are you bitten?" asks Caius.

"Ash came," I tell him. "He said he believes I wanted him to die. He thinks I was competing with him—that our friendship has been about winning. He said he wants me gone forever."

Caius shines the flashlight well over me. He feels of my arms, hands, and legs—places likely for a fox to nip. He seems satisfied for the moment.

"He dumped at my feet everything I'd left at his house," I tell Caius.

"Let's get you on home." Caius takes me by the elbows and leads me to my feet.

I look up at him.

"Except for my books."

I can picture all of them, strewn in a messy pile on Ash's living room floor, where we last looked at them.

"He kept them, but he's refusing to admit that he has them."

"We'll see about that," says Caius.

I pull out from beneath his arm.

"Cockle shards."

Caius stops. "What?"

"I wasn't supposed to tell anyone that. He said accusing him of lying would make me all the more a bad person."

Caius settles his arm again around my shoulders. "Don't think on him twice, Swift. You're done with him."

I don't want to be done with him—but of course Caius knows this.

And I know what Caius is thinking. I can't stop this change from coming.

My chest aches with the fact that Ash's family is breaking. That Caius is leaving. That I've lost every book that I have.

Except one.

I can feel the heaviness of *The Star of Atlantis* in my rucksack, loaded as it is with legends of treasure and the hopeful assurance that lost things might not always be lost. Despite that things change.

Walking through our Oak Empire—heavy with our memories, even now, cloaked by this darkness; passing the relics of my childhood with Ash; my skin scented warm by the wildness of the fox; my shoulders soothed beneath the arm of my brother who will soon disappear—I strain to see the pathway before us.

Even with the flashlight beaming, our sightline of the trail remains shallow, and the going feels rougher.

The world seems to have shifted somehow, like a bike clicked into a higher gear.

But training my gaze up toward the crowns of the ancient trees, to where the mist thins, I still see the strengthening stars.

THE END

SWIFT'S JOURNEY CONTINUES

Swift & The Star of Atlantis Series

A starry-eyed boy. A cryptic map. A mythical treasure.

What perils await in the chasing of dreams?

As Swift lives up to his name and his family legacy, young adults receive a fast-paced fantasy that will appeal not just on the adventure or fantasy levels, but in matters of the heart as the young struggle for independence and action in the face of parental restrictions. Tricia D. Wagner's attention to pairing psychological struggle with the adventure of finding a promised treasure creates a story that pulls on the emotions of young readers as it satisfies their desire for action and adventure.

-D. Donovan, Senior Reviewer, *Midwest Book Review*

Where Fish Can Breathe

Ten-year-old Swift longs to be as grown up as his brothers, but in confronting himself in the wilds of the North Atlantic, he must contend with what it means to be a man.

SEA OF GLASS

WHEN AN OLD ANGLER PRESSES TEO TO SEEK A GODDESS—THE SEA ANGEL—FOR RESCUE, TEO SETS OUT ALONG BAJA'S WILD COAST TO TEST WHETHER HELP CAN BE FOUND AT THE HANDS OF THE GODS.

TO LEARN THE TRUTH, HE MUST LOOK BEYOND LEGENDS AND SUMMON THE COURAGE TO CHALLENGE HIS PAPÁ.

AND TO REACH FREEDOM, HE MUST TAP HIS OWN STRENGTH, HIDDEN BENEATH WOUNDS LAID BY GLASS.

About the Author

Tricia D. Wagner is an award-winning novelist, poet, and short story writer. She grew up in Amarillo, Texas, chasing storms, riding stallions, sojourning through painted canyons, disappearing into floating mesas under starry skies.

She now lives in Rockford, Illinois (though the truth is, she's a citizen of a dozen fictional countries). Tricia works in education and lives day to day wonderstruck but luckily can feel her way about this terrifying, beautiful Earth through writing.

Tricia has pieces published in the *Write City Magazine*, *Chicago Newa*, *Word of Art 3D*, *Literary Yard*, and *Midwest Review*.

Author's Note

I love connecting with readers and writers. If, you're interested in stories, then you're a kindred spirit to me, and I have lots more in store for you.

To quote another kindred spirit in writing, Jedi Master Stephen King:

"Writing is magic, as much as the water of life as any other art. The water is free. So drink. Drink and be filled up."

If you're interested not only in stories, but in story creation, visit my website and sign up to receive a **FREE Story Kickoff Character Worksheet.**

I designed this tool for that first moment of getting our feet wet at the brink of a story.

To get your FREE worksheet, visit:
www.TriciaWagner.com